THE JOURNEY OF TWO DECADES ON EARTH

RIZALY SIDDIQ

To all who are reading and will read,.

Contents

FOREWORD

"The Journey of Two Decades on Earth" offers a thoughtful and insightful view of the world, drawn from my experiences and observations over several decades. This guidebook is designed to provide guidance and support to those in their first two decades of life, a critical period that shapes our values, relationships, and future paths.

As we navigate the complexities of growing up, it's easy to feel overwhelmed by the challenges and uncertainties that lie ahead. But with the right mindset, support, and guidance, we can turn these obstacles into opportunities for growth, learning, and self-discovery.

Through its pages, I hope to inspire and encourage you to embark on your own journey of self-discovery, navigating the challenges and opportunities that lie ahead. Whether you're facing questions about your identity, relationships, or future goals, this guidebook aims to provide you with valuable insights, practical advice, and inspiration to help you find your way.

Preface

As I sit down to write this book, I am filled with a sense of purpose and responsibility. The first two decades of our lives are a critical period that lays the foundation for who we become. It is a time of discovery, growth, and exploration.

Through this book, I hope to share my insights, and lessons learned, in the hope that they may provide guidance and support to those navigating this critical period. I believe that by sharing experiences, we can learn from each other and grow together.

ACKNOWLEDGEMENTS

I would like to thank my grandparents for making me what I am today. I would like to express my gratitude to my parents for providing me with everything. They have never said 'no' when it comes to me. I really thank them for raising me as a good child.

I would like to thank my uncle and aunt for showing me endless love.

I would like to thank my teachers, who are responsible for every good thought I gained throughout the years.

I would like to thank my brothers for setting my standards very high.

I would like to thank my sisters for making me a little kind.

I would like to thank my friends who supported me in every situation.

I heartily thank myself for being able to complete my first book, on which I have worked for a significant interval of time.

I would like to thank my readers for choosing me and my art. Being a writer is not easy. Your support means a lot to me.

I heartily thank Notion Press for publishing this masterpiece and trusting my work.

Without you people and my consistency, this book would have never been born.

I would like to express my gratitude to all who've joined me on this journey through words. May the connections we've made through language stay with us forever.

"To all who is reading and who will read!"

Prologue

What is life? Is there anyone who can answer? Who is leading us? The answer is: Undefined.

To me, life is a journey shaped by our experiences, observations, and interactions with others. The first two decades of our lives lay the foundation for who we become. It's a critical period that influences our values, relationships, and future paths.

A healthy beginning, built on positive experiences and lessons learned, is essential for navigating life's challenges. According to me, our life is unorganized, and we live by observing others. Most of everything that defines us is shaped in the first two decades; it is only responsible for what we are!

We come across people all over our lives, but the beginning is here only. It is essential to have a healthy beginning.

And so, our journey begins...

In the pathway we've voyaged, though often unobserved, we shall unearth their beauty in the upcoming pages...

What's possibly in? Just 20 years in everyone's life... but wait! Just 20 years?! Isn't it underrated? From happiness to depression, and all the emotions in between, we've walked through this journey! Let us revisit some of its pivotal moments...

I
THE SPARK OF LIFE

The Journey Begins

Life's odyssey starts with a mysterious, unforgettable moment – our birth. Though we may not recall it, our loved ones' faces light up with joy. As we grow, time transforms us dramatically. We outgrow our parents' arms, our clothes, and our childhood. With each milestone – sitting, standing, walking, and running – we captivate those around us.

Embracing Life's Ups and Downs

We learn, we fall, and we rise again. As we explore our surroundings, we mimic the actions of those around us. These early experiences shape us, defining who we become. As we navigate life, we encounter solitude, shared love, and new relationships. We discover ourselves, our passions, and our strengths.

Decade of Discovery

Our first decade brings the magic of school and friendships. The second decade challenges our assumptions, helping us grow. By the end of it, we've gathered experiences that help us define life.

Walking Through Life's Pages

Join me on this journey through life's amusing, confusing, and enlightening moments. How long will life's winding path keep us engaged? It's okay to encounter darkness; be the light that guides you.

Happy Beginning!

As we embark on this extraordinary adventure, we begin to realize that life is a masterpiece of moments, each one a brushstroke on the canvas of our existence. With every step, we weave the threads of experience, wisdom, and love into a rich and intricate narrative that shapes us into the individuals we're meant to be. And so, as we walk through life's pages, let us cherish the spark that ignites our journey, nurture the flame that fuels our passions, and radiate the light that guides us forward.

II
THE EARLY LESSONS

Laying the Foundation: The First Decade's Lasting Impact

Our first ten years of life are a treasure trove of unconditional love and acceptance. This pivotal decade shapes our expectations and lays the groundwork for who we become. Every experience, every triumph, and every struggle during this period reflects in our lives today, tomorrow, and beyond.

Navigating the Turbulent Teens: Discovery and Growth

As we enter our second decade, curiosity gets the better of us. We're fascinated by the world around us, and our experiences shape us in profound ways. This decade can be confusing, but with patience and perseverance, it can also lead us to the path of success.

Embracing Life's Twists and Turns

During this stage, we may encounter unexpected challenges. Even those who loved us unconditionally may occasionally withdraw their affection, leaving us feeling lost and vulnerable. We may face drastic changes that push us out of our comfort zones. Yet, these experiences can ultimately enrich our lives.

Finding Hope and Positivity in Life's Ups and Downs

It's easy to get bogged down by disappointments, like boring school days or disappointing grades. However, we mustn't lose sight of the bigger picture. Happiness and interest can be found in the simplest things. Amidst life's turbulence, we must focus on the positive. Hope is the key to unlocking our potential.

Chasing Dreams and Aspirations

As we navigate life's journey, our dreams and aspirations evolve. We begin to discover our passions and interests, and our hopes for the future start to take shape. We learn to set goals, work towards them, and celebrate our achievements.

Overcoming Obstacles and Staying Resilient

Life's journey is not without its challenges. We face obstacles, setbacks, and failures, but it's how we respond that matters. We learn to pick ourselves up, dust ourselves off, and keep moving forward. With each setback, we grow stronger, wiser, and more resilient.

The Power of Relationships in Shaping Our Lives

Throughout our lives, relationships play a vital role in shaping who we become. Our family, friends, and community support us, guide us, and help us grow. As we navigate life's ups and downs, these relationships become our rock, our safe haven.

Unraveling the Mystery of Self-Discovery

As we grow, we begin to uncover our true selves. We discover our strengths, our weaknesses, and our passions. We learn to love ourselves, flaws and all, and we develop a sense of purpose and direction.

Reflecting on Life's Journey So Far

As we reflect on life's early chapters, we begin to realize that the experiences, relationships, and lessons we've accumulated are merely the foundation upon which we'll build the rest of our lives. But as we look to the future, we're confronted with a profound question: "Will we continue to write our story with the same pen, or will we dare to pick up a new one and create a masterpiece?" The answer whispers in the wind, a gentle breeze that rustles the pages of our soul.

III

EDUCATION - IS ALSO A BASIC NEED

What is the value of knowledge if it is not accompanied by the wisdom to use it with kindness, empathy, and compassion? A person may possess vast amounts of information, but if they lack respect for others, they are ultimately a failure. On the other hand, individuals who have learned manners, respect, and social responsibility are truly educated, for they possess the tools to build strong relationships, foster positive change, and create a lasting impact on the world.

A Lifelong Journey

Through this journey, we come to understand that education is not just about ourselves, but also about how we impact others. We learn to love, to care, and to compassionately connect with those around us. We develop empathy, kindness, and generosity, becoming beacons of hope and positivity in our communities. As we continue on this path, we realize that education is a lifelong journey, not a destination.

A Final Awakening

Remember that the journey of learning is a lifelong odyssey. It's a path that winds through triumphs and tribulations, shaping us into compassionate, resilient, and empowered individuals. Will you answer the call to embark on this transformative journey? Will you harness the power of education to create a brighter, more compassionate world? The choice is yours. The future is waiting.

IV
MISTAKES - LEARNING AND OUTCOMES

The Beauty of Mistakes

What lies beneath the notion of mistakes? Is it merely an error in judgment, a miscalculation, or a misstep? Or is it something more profound - a reflection of our limitations, a measure of our growth, or a test of our resilience? As we ponder these questions, we begin to realize that mistakes are an inherent part of the human experience.

Mistakes as Catalysts for Growth and Transformation

Mistakes play a crucial role in shaping our identities, influencing our choices, and informing our understanding of success and failure. Through mistakes, we gain invaluable knowledge and insight, often more profound than any achievement or success. Interestingly, we tend to remember our mistakes more vividly than our accomplishments, a testament to the lasting impact they have on our lives.

Consequently, it's in the quagmire of our mistakes that we discover our greatest strengths, learning to navigate the complexities of life and emerging stronger, wiser, and more resilient with each passing day. Learning and outcome: the more we learn, the more we grow, but paradoxically, the more mistakes we make, the more we learn.

This realization puts us all on a never-ending journey of discovery, where the destination is undefined, and the journey itself becomes the art. We are the artists, navigating the complexities of life, making mistakes, and uncovering new truths. In this beautiful mess, we find growth, wisdom, and the courage to continue creating.

The art of mistake-making is the alchemy of turning failure into wisdom, where the raw materials of error are transmuted into the gold of knowledge. By embracing the process of trial and error, we tap into the deepest sources of wisdom, where the boundaries between mistake and mastery blur, and the music of our experiences becomes the harmony of our growth.

In the grand tapestry of human experience, mistakes are the threads that weave together growth, learning, and transformation. In conclusion, mistakes are an integral part of our journey, serving as catalysts for growth, learning, and transformation. The most important lesson we can glean from mistakes is that they are not failures, but opportunities for growth and transformation. Through our mistakes, we gain invaluable knowledge, develop resilience, and uncover our greatest strengths. So, let's make mistakes together, learn and grow, for the future well-being of ourselves! In the world of uncertainty, let's live!

V
THE HOPE IN YOU - YOU MUST HAVE

Hope is indeed not simple; it's a complex and multifaceted concept that illuminates our path, even in the darkest of times. A ray of hope can be the difference between giving up and persevering, between despair and resilience. Moreover, hope inspires us to take action, motivates us to strive for excellence, and ultimately, propels us to push beyond our limits.

Our goals, dreams, and aspirations rely on hope to transport us to a world of possibilities, where anything can happen and miracles are within reach. With hope, we're empowered to take the first step, despite uncertainty or potential failure, and it's through this process that we learn and grow. Hope ignites our passions, creativity, and motivation, propelling us forward like a phoenix rising from the ashes.

Hope is like a miracle that can revive a life, underlies our experiences, relationships, and memories, giving us a sense of purpose and meaning. Sharing hope with loved ones supports and uplifts them, helping them stay focused on their goals. It reminds us that we're not alone in our journey and that together, we can overcome daunting challenges.

In today's world, where challenges and uncertainties abound, hope is more essential than ever. We must cultivate and nurture hope in ourselves and those around us, ensuring we have a maximum level of hope to carry us through life's ups and downs. By embracing hope, we create a ripple effect of positivity, inspiring others to do the same. As the Japanese proverb goes, "Fall down seven times, stand up eight." Hope gives us the strength to stand up, keep moving forward, and never give up on our dreams.

Hope gives us permission to make mistakes and learn from them. With hope, we're more willing to take risks, experiment, and innovate. Through trial and error, we learn, grow, and refine our skills. Hope resonates deeply with the concept of "kaizen" – the Japanese philosophy of continuous improvement. Kaizen emphasizes taking small steps towards improvement, learning from mistakes, and persisting through challenges.

May hope be the guiding force that illuminates our journey, inspiring us to persevere, to grow, and to thrive. May its transformative power ignite our passions, fuel our creativity, and propel us towards our dreams. And may we share this precious gift with others, creating a world where hope and positivity flourish.

VI
FRIENDS AND FAMILY

Friends and family – two vital components of our lives that not only share a common starting letter but also mirror each other's roles. A mother's nurturing, a father's protection, a grandma's loving care, and a grandpa's wisdom all contribute to our growth.

Siblings share their favorite things and create lifelong memories, while uncles and aunts show unexpected care and thoughtfulness. However, what sets friends apart is that they provide all these things and more – a constant source of support, comfort, and camaraderie.

In many ways, friends become the family we choose, offering a sense of belonging and connection that's just as strong. As the ancient Greek philosopher Aristotle said, "What is a friend? A single soul dwelling in two bodies." This profound statement highlights the deep emotional connection we share with our loved ones.

Our relationships with family and friends are a manifestation of the human need for connection, love, and belonging. In the spirit of Ubuntu, we recognize that our humanity is tied to the humanity of others. We are because they are.

This interconnectedness is beautifully illustrated by the concept of "sonder," which reminds us that every person we encounter has a unique story, struggle, and beauty. As we navigate the complexities of life, we come to realize that our relationships are not just a source of comfort but also a catalyst for personal growth.

Through our interactions with others, we discover new aspects of ourselves, develop empathy, and cultivate a deeper understanding of the world. The bittersweet longing of Saudade reminds us to appreciate the preciousness of our time with loved ones and to nurture these relationships with empathy, kindness, and compassion.

As we look back on our lives, we realize that it's the connections we make that give life its meaning. Compassion is the melody that orchestrates our shared existence, harmonizing our differences and synchronizing our hearts.

The importance of family cannot be overstated. We all have families, and despite the ups and downs, excitements, and disappointments, we feel complete with them. We never choose our family, nor do they choose us, but still, we are together, and that is the greatest blessing.

This truth applies to every living organism; being together is nature's design for everything that has life. Apart from family, we have surroundings, neighbors, friends, and pets that can enrich our lives. A healthy environment can make all the difference, allowing us to thrive and grow.

Yet, even if we're not blessed with ideal circumstances or face disappointments along the way, we mustn't give up. We should rise above, explore every opportunity, and trust that at some destined point, we will receive what we deserve – everything beneath the roof called sky!

In our selfless moments, we often put others' needs before our own, especially when it comes to our beloved family and friends. At some point, we catch a glimpse of hope and feel an overwhelming desire to live for them, to build a life together, and to create a home that we've always dreamed of – a sanctuary filled with love, laughter, and warmth.

So, let us cherish and nurture these relationships, recognizing the profound impact they have on our lives and the people we're becoming. Perhaps our beginnings may be imperfect, but as we grow, it becomes our duty to learn from our mistakes, correct our paths, and strive to create a brighter, more loving future – not just for ourselves, but for all.

By doing so, we can truly live and let live, cultivating a world where compassion, empathy, and kindness thrive. Even if we are not so blessed or feel some disappointments at any point or at every point, we should go up and explore everything we could. Maybe at any destined point, we will get what we deserve, and we deserve everything beneath the roof called sky!

As we spread good vibes in our surroundings, we embark on a transformative journey. With each new connection, we not only get to know others but also discover more about ourselves. Let us travel to the next outstanding page of life, where every experience is an opportunity to learn, grow, and evolve.

VII
BUILDING MEANINGFUL RELATIONSHIPS

The Foundation of Meaningful Relationships

It all begins with a spark of mutual respect. When we find that special someone, our connection ignites, fueled by a deep admiration for each other's unique essence. Respect: The North Star of Relationships, guides us, keeping our bond strong.

Stay True to Your Roots

When we start with mutual respect, we must stay committed to that same energy. We shouldn't compromise our values or change who we are to fit someone else's mold. Instead, we should celebrate our individuality and honor the qualities that make us unique.

The Power of Consistency

By staying true to ourselves and our values, we create a sense of consistency and reliability in our relationships. This, in turn, fosters trust, understanding, and a deeper connection with our partner.

Transformative Takeaway

Remember, meaningful relationships are built on mutual respect, trust, and consistency. By staying true to ourselves and our values, we can create a connection that's authentic, empowering, and transformative.

Types of Relationships

1. Romantic Relationships: Intimate partnerships between two individuals, often characterized by emotional and physical connection.
2. Familial Relationships: Connections between family members, such as parents, siblings, and extended family.
3. Platonic Relationships: Close friendships between individuals, often sharing common interests and experiences.
4. Professional Relationships: Connections between colleagues, mentors, and peers in a work or academic setting.
5. Social Relationships: Casual connections with acquaintances, community members, or social networks.

The Blurred Lines of Perception

We often misinterpret our own emotions and those of others, especially when we're caught up in the excitement of a new connection. This misperception can lead to unrealistic expectations, misunderstandings, and ultimately, hurt.

The Mutual Dance of Hurt

"The art of getting hurt and hurting others begins mutually." This poignant phrase acknowledges that hurt is often a two-way street. When we're not mindful of our own emotions and boundaries, we can unintentionally hurt others, and vice versa.

The Importance of Self-Awareness and Communication

To navigate these complex dynamics, it's essential to cultivate self-awareness, empathy, and open communication. By recognizing our own emotions and limitations, we can better understand others and build more resilient, compassionate relationships.

Why do conflicts arise in relationships we've chosen?

We thought we'd found the perfect match, but somehow, things didn't go as planned. Meaningful relationships start with mutual respect. When we find that special someone, we must stay true to ourselves and our values. We often misunderstand ourselves and others, especially when we feel good. But if things don't go as expected, it can lead to hurt. The problem starts with us and ultimately ends with others. We want others to satisfy our expectations, but we're not capable of doing that ourselves. The way we are should be what we want others to be. The more we expect, the more hurt we'll feel. Don't search for the standard in others, be the standard yourself, and you'll attract your significant mind. It's time to shift our focus inward and work on becoming the best version of ourselves. By doing so, we'll naturally attract someone who resonates with our energy and values.

What is the ultimate cause of breakage in relationships? Is it the lack of love, the absence of trust, or something deeper?

Relationships - the beautiful dance of two souls, bound together by love, trust, and understanding. But, what happens when the rhythm falters, and the harmony turns to discord?

The Cracks Begin to Show

Misunderstandings creep in, like thieves in the night, stealing away the joy and laughter. The lack of quality time together becomes a chasm, ever-widening, until the connection is lost.

As problems arise, we often Hit the Panic Button, wanting to escape the turmoil rather than face the music. But, in doing so, we risk Missing the Beat, losing the opportunity to strengthen our bond and deepen our love.

The Plot Twist

External influences can throw a wrench in the works, making us question our commitment and loyalty. But, here's the thing: If It's Meant to Be, It Will Be. No matter what comes our way, our love will shine through, like a beacon in the darkness.

So, what's the takeaway?

The Bitter Truth

Relationships require effort, patience, and understanding. We must be willing to Face the Music, acknowledging our flaws and working to overcome them.

The Final Act

Rather than engaging in Cold Wars, let's choose to Communicate, Not Hate. By doing so, we'll create a love that's Stronger Than Yesterday, a bond that will weather any storm.

Traumas of relationships - the unseen scars that linger long after the heartbreak. Are you haunted by the memories of a past relationship? Do the wounds still feel fresh, the pain still echoing through your mind?

The Blame Game - A Dangerous Dance: We often get stuck in the blame game, replaying the hurts of the past like a broken record. We forget that There Are Always Two Sides to the Story. In our quest for validation, we neglect to acknowledge the harm we may have caused. It's time to break free from this toxic cycle.

The Ripple Effect - How Pain Can Poison: When we hold onto past hurts, we start to Reflect the Pain, unconsciously hurting those around us. It's a vicious cycle, where we seek revenge or validation for our own suffering. But The Past Does Not Define Us. We have the power to choose a different path.

From Hurt to Healing - A Journey of Self-Discovery: So, how do we move forward? By Facing the Music, acknowledging our flaws, and taking responsibility for our actions. It's time to Shatter the Illusions of the past and Embrace the Truth. By doing so, we'll unlock the door to personal growth, healing, and a brighter future.

The Future Awaits: Will You Answer? Will you continue to let the traumas of past relationships haunt you, or will you choose to break free? The power is yours. Take the First Step, and embark on a journey of self-discovery, healing, and transformation.

In the depths of human connection, where love, trust, and vulnerability entwine, a profound question echoes: Will you dare to unravel the mysteries of your heart, and in doing so, become the masterpiece you've been searching for? That's a question that has puzzled many for centuries. Some say the answer lies within, while others claim it's hidden in the whispers of the universe. But perhaps the answer begins with embracing the imperfect, the imperfect us. Dive into the beauty of imperfection and discover the freedom that comes with it.

VIII
EMBRACING IMPERFECTIONS

Imperfections are an inherent part of our existence. We're often conditioned to strive for perfection, to conceal our flaws and present a polished exterior. But the truth is, perfection is an unattainable ideal. Every person, every experience, and every moment is uniquely flawed.

Rather than trying to achieve an unrealistic standard, let's learn to appreciate the beauty of imperfection. Our quirks, flaws, and imperfections make us who we are, and they're what make life worth living. By embracing our authentic selves, we'll find freedom from the pressure to conform and discover a more genuine way of living.

Self-acceptance is the key to unlocking our true potential. When we love and accept ourselves, flaws and all, we open ourselves up to growth, learning, and meaningful connections with others.

what are imperfection?

Imperfections are the essence of our humanity. They're the scars that tell stories of our past, the quirks that make us uniquely us, and the fears that remind us we're vulnerable. Imperfections are the unplanned detours that lead us to new discoveries, the mistakes that teach us valuable lessons, and the uncertainties that keep us grounded.

They're the imperfections in our appearance, the flaws in our character, and the frailties in our relationships. Imperfections are the memories we cherish, the experiences that shape us, and the moments that make life worth living.

In every imperfection, there's a story, a lesson, and a beauty that makes us who we are.

When we're made to feel imperfect because of our appearance, remember that everyone is unique. No one can be the most beautiful; no one is ugly. We're all real.

If imperfection is our performance, consider that we're human, not AI. Even AI has its unique strengths. No one is a topper or average; we all perform with our interests and do our utmost best – not someone else's.

If imperfection is our status, none of us deserve it. We only know the present, but in the past, we were all just a few atoms.

So, if imperfection is in our actions, let's kindly embrace it. Help yourself by acknowledging that imperfections are a natural part of being human.

During moments of mental breakdown, remember:

You're not here to satisfy others' expectations; your worth isn't defined by external validation.

Don't look down on yourself; your struggles don't diminish your value or identity.

The way you are, in this moment, is enough. Your uniqueness, strengths, and weaknesses make you who you are.

Keep working on improving yourself, not for others, but for your own growth and well-being.

Be gentle with yourself, and acknowledge that it's okay to not be okay.

Embracing the Art of Acceptance

Be satisfied with what you have – mentally, physically, socially, and financially. The more you accept yourself, the more you'll grow.

Start with self-acceptance, then extend it to others. Recognize that everyone has flaws and imperfections.

Treat others with respect and equality. Remember, everyone deserves the same kindness and compassion you offer to yourself.

Practice mindfulness and self-care. Take care of your physical, emotional, and mental well-being.

Apply the Golden Rule: what you give to others, give to yourself first. What you expect from others, satisfy those expectations within yourself.

The art of acceptance can transform your life. By embracing your imperfections and those of others, you'll find peace, compassion, and understanding.

Overcome the fear of vulnerability by being your authentic self. Don't change who you are to please others.

Life is a rollercoaster with ups and downs, but it's uniquely yours. Don't try to alter its course unless it's for your own growth and well-being.

Celebrate all forms of imperfection and find satisfaction in being yourself.

Remember, you can only do for yourself what others cannot. Don't rely on others to make changes or improvements in your life. Take ownership and do it for yourself.

Similarly, don't try to change or improve others. Focus on your own growth and development. You can't force others to change, but you can control your own actions and decisions."

"Do for yourself, not for others. Your growth, your change, your decision." and for others just say "No"

IX
THE ART OF SAYING NO

Saying no can be one of the most empowering words in our vocabulary. Yet, it's often the hardest word to utter. We're conditioned to prioritize others' needs, avoid conflict, and seek approval. But constantly saying yes can lead to burnout, resentment, and a loss of identity.

The art of saying no is not about being confrontational or dismissive; it's about being intentional, assertive, and honest. It's about recognizing that every yes requires a corresponding no, and that saying no can be a powerful act of self-care and self-love. we'll explore the transformative power of saying no, and provide practical guidance on how to do it with confidence, compassion, and clarity.

Saying no is not a negative act, but a positive one. It's a declaration of self-awareness, self-respect, and self-love. When you say no, you're saying yes to yourself, your values, and your priorities.

However, saying no can be challenging, especially when:
- You fear disappointing or hurting others
- You're afraid of missing out (FOMO)
- You're pressured by societal expectations or norms
- You're unsure of your own boundaries or priorities

To overcome these challenges, it's essential to develop a deeper understanding of yourself, your values, and your limits.

A Harmonious Balance of Self and Universe : The Four Pillars of Saying No

In the words of ancient Greek philosopher, Heraclitus, "The way up and the way down are one and the same." Saying no can be a powerful act of self-love, self-respect, and self-care, yet it can also be challenging. By embracing the universal concepts of harmony, balance, and self-awareness, we can develop a deeper understanding of the art of saying no.

Self-Awareness: Know Thyself

The ancient Greek aphorism "Know Thyself" is inscribed at the Temple of Apollo at Delphi. To say no with confidence, you must first know yourself. This includes understanding your values, desires, and limits. The universe is a mirror, reflecting your inner world. By developing self-awareness, you'll become more mindful of your vibrational frequency and attract experiences that align with your true nature.

Setting Boundaries: The Principle of Non-Contradiction

Aristotle's Principle of Non-Contradiction states that something cannot both be and not be at the same time. Similarly, setting healthy boundaries requires recognizing what you are and are not willing to accept. By establishing clear boundaries, you'll create a harmonious balance between your inner and outer worlds.

Overcoming Obstacles

The Concept of Enantiodromia : Enantiodromia, a concept developed by Heraclitus, describes the process of something turning into its opposite. When faced with obstacles, remember that every challenge has the potential to become an opportunity for growth. By embracing this concept, you'll develop the resilience to overcome obstacles and say no with confidence.

Assertive Communication: The Power of Logos

In ancient Greek philosophy, Logos refers to the power of reason, logic, and communication. Saying no assertively requires speaking your truth with confidence, clarity, and respect. By harnessing the power of Logos, you'll communicate your boundaries effectively and maintain harmonious relationships.

The art of saying no is not just about setting boundaries or asserting yourself; it's about understanding the universal principles that govern our reality. By embracing self-awareness, setting healthy boundaries, overcoming obstacles, and communicating assertively, you'll master the art of saying no and unlock a more authentic, empowered you!

X

THE REPLACEMENTS - THE FRAGILITY OF HUMAN CONNECTION

Replacement is a common phenomenon in our daily lives, where we substitute one thing for another to fill a void, satisfy a need, or alleviate discomfort. This can be seen in our interactions with material objects, where we replace old or broken items with new ones. For instance, when our phones are no longer functional, we replace them with newer models.

The Replacement Paradox: Is it Fair to Replace a Human Connection? However, when it comes to human relationships, replacement takes on a different connotation. As one observer notes, "Replacements occur, but it's not a qualitative approach. Can someone replace the place of others? Is it fair? But it happens! People value others differently, and relationships are temporary. I've witnessed important people becoming strangers, and strangers becoming important. Replacements happen, but why so fast, in such a hurry?"

Choosing Connection Over Replacement

We live in a world where replacement is a common phenomenon. But when it comes to human connections, is replacement really an option? Let's be clear: choosing to like someone and be with them is a choice. It's a spark that ignites a connection. But staying with them – through life's ups and downs – is a decision. A decision that requires dedication, effort, and vulnerability.

It's a commitment to navigate the depths of human emotion, to laugh, cry, and grow together. And it's this decision that separates fleeting connections from meaningful relationships. But what happens when we replace someone? Do we truly find a suitable substitute? Or are we simply trying to fill a void that may never be fully filled?

The Irreplaceability of Human Connections

The truth is, every human connection is irreplaceable. Each person brings their own experiences, perspectives, and emotions to the table. When we replace someone, we're not just losing a relationship – we're losing a part of ourselves. So, is it fair to replace a human connection? The answer is clear: no.

When we stay with someone, we're not just maintaining a relationship – we're cultivating a deeper understanding of ourselves and others. Replacement may be a common phenomenon, but it's not a solution for meaningful connections. It's time to recognize the value of commitment and the irreplaceability of human relationships.

The Fleeting Nature of Friendships

While relationships are often scrutinized for their impermanence, friendships are equally vulnerable to the phenomenon of replacement. In today's fast-paced world, people are increasingly prone to abandoning existing friendships in pursuit of newer, seemingly better connections.

This trend is alarming, as it suggests that friendships are disposable and lacking in depth. When individuals prioritize finding "better" friends over nurturing existing relationships, they undermine the very foundation of friendship.

The Importance of Loyalty and Commitment

Friendships are built on shared experiences, trust, and emotional investment. They require effort, empathy, and understanding to flourish. However, when people view friendships as interchangeable, they neglect the value of these meaningful connections.

This "upgrade" mentality can lead to a never-ending cycle of replacement, where individuals constantly seek new friendships, only to discard them when something "better" comes along. This not only harms those who are replaced but also prevents individuals from forming deep, lasting connections.

A Call to Action

Let's not treat people like disposable objects, causing emotional pollution. Just as we strive to reduce waste, let's cultivate empathy and compassion to build meaningful connections.

Let's not forget the hands that served us in our darkest times. Our parents, grandparents, friends, and loved ones who stood by us when we had nothing, deserve our care and support when they need it most. Abandoning them in their time of need is not only a betrayal, but also a crime.

Let's reciprocate their kindness and be there for them when they need us most. It's what makes us human....

XI
THE IMPACT OF SOCIAL MEDIA

In today's interconnected world, social media has emerged as a powerful tool, bridging gaps and fostering global connections like never before. By revolutionizing the way we communicate, share ideas, and build relationships, social media has opened doors to new opportunities and experiences, forever changing the fabric of modern life.

Social media has a profound impact on our lives, extending far beyond its entertaining and useful features. While it can be a fun and engaging way to connect with others, it also consumes our time and can have severe consequences on our mental and physical health.

Moreover, social media can be a source of trouble, not only within our homes but also within ourselves. It's like a clever kidnapper, luring us in with enticing treats before taking hold of our lives. The constant stream of information and notifications can lead to addiction, eroding our mental clarity and diminishing our quality of life.

Mental Health Concerns

Social media can have a profound impact on our mental health, contributing to increased levels of anxiety, depression, and loneliness. Some of the ways social media can affect mental health include:

- Comparison and decreased self-esteem: Social media platforms showcase the highlight reels of other people's lives, making it easy to compare and feel inferior.

- Fear of missing out (FOMO): The constant stream of updates can create a sense of FOMO, leading to feelings of anxiety and stress.

- Cyberbullying and online harassment: Social media can be a breeding ground for bullying and harassment, which can have serious negative effects on mental health.

- Sleep deprivation: Exposure to screens and the constant notifications from social media can interfere with sleep patterns, leading to sleep deprivation and related mental health issues.

Impact on Relationships

Excessive social media use can also strain relationships with family and friends. Some of the ways social media can impact relationships include:

- Social comparison and decreased empathy: Social media can make us more focused on our own lives and less empathetic towards others.

- Decreased face-to-face interaction: Spending too much time on social media can lead to decreased face-to-face interaction, which is essential for building and maintaining strong relationships.

- Miscommunication and misunderstandings: Social media can also lead to miscommunication and misunderstandings, which can strain relationships.

- Unrealistic expectations: Social media can create unrealistic expectations about relationships, leading to disappointment and frustration.

Effects on Physical Health

Finally, social media can also have negative effects on physical health, including:

- Sedentary lifestyle: Spending too much time on social media can lead to a sedentary lifestyle, which is linked to a range of physical health problems.

- Sleep deprivation: As mentioned earlier, social media can interfere with sleep patterns, leading to sleep deprivation and related physical health issues.

- Poor nutrition: Social media can also lead to poor nutrition, as people spend more time scrolling through their feeds and less time preparing healthy meals.

- Increased risk of chronic diseases: Excessive social media use has been linked to an increased risk of chronic diseases, including heart disease, diabetes, and obesity.

Some Sweet Solutions and Strategies

Maintaining a Healthy Balance

To mitigate the negative effects of social media, it's essential to establish a healthy balance between online and offline activities. Here are some strategies to help you achieve this balance:

1. Set boundaries: Establish specific times for social media use, and stick to those times. For example, you might allow yourself to check social media only after you've completed a task or reached a specific milestone.

2. Use website blockers: Use tools that can block social media sites or other distracting websites during certain periods of the day.

3. Schedule social media-free times: Designate specific times of the day or week as social media-free. For example, you might decide not to use social media during meals, during family time, or on Sundays.

4. Replace social media with offline activities: Engage in hobbies, exercise, or creative pursuits that bring you joy and fulfillment.

5. Practice mindfulness: Regular mindfulness practice can help you become more aware of your social media use and reduce mindless scrolling.

The Importance of Digital Literacy

Digital literacy is critical in today's digital age. It's essential to educate ourselves and others on responsible social media use, online safety, and digital etiquette. Here are some key aspects of digital literacy:

1. Online safety: Understand how to protect yourself from cyberbullying, online harassment, and identity theft.

2. Digital etiquette: Learn how to communicate respectfully and responsibly online, including how to avoid spreading misinformation or engaging in online conflicts.

3. Media literacy: Develop critical thinking skills to evaluate the credibility of online sources and identify biased or misleading information.

4. Responsible social media use: Understand how to use social media in a way that promotes positive relationships, self-esteem, and mental health.

social media is a complex and multifaceted phenomenon that presents both benefits and drawbacks. On the one hand, social media has revolutionized the way we communicate, connect, and share information. It has enabled us to build global communities, access vast amounts of knowledge, and express ourselves in new and creative ways.On the other hand, excessive social media use has been linked to a range of negative consequences, including mental health concerns, social isolation, and decreased attention span. It's clear that social media is a double-edged sword, offering both opportunities and risks.

As individuals, it's essential that we're mindful of our social media use and its potential consequences. We must take responsibility for our own social media habits, recognizing when we're using these platforms in ways that are detrimental to our well-being. By being more intentional and discerning in our social media use, we can harness the benefits of these platforms while minimizing their risks.

So what can you do to promote a healthier balance in your social media use? Take a moment to reflect on your own habits and consider making a few simple changes. Set boundaries around your social media use, prioritize offline activities, and cultivate meaningful relationships with others. By taking control of your social media use, you can create a more balanced, fulfilling, and connected life.

Remember, social media is a tool, not a substitute for human connection. By using these platforms responsibly and mindfully, we can unlock their full potential while preserving our mental, emotional, and relational well-being.

As we've seen how social media shapes our relationships and perceptions, let's now explore another fundamental aspect of human experience: expectation. How do our expectations influence our lives, and what can we learn from this complex and multifaceted concept?

XII

EXPECTATION : THE BEAUTIFUL ENIGMA

In the pursuit of happiness and fulfillment, we often find ourselves entangled in a web of expectations. The ancient Greeks spoke of "Eudaimonia," a state of being that encompasses living a life of happiness, fulfillment, and flourishing. This concept suggests that our expectations should be aligned with our values, goals, and aspirations. When we strive for Eudaimonia, we're more likely to set expectations that are realistic, achievable, and fulfilling.

As we navigate the complexities of expectation, we begin to realize that it's a double-edged sword. On one hand, expectation can fuel our passions, motivate us to strive for excellence, and inspire us to reach for the impossible. On the other hand, unmet expectations can lead to disappointment, disillusionment, and even despair.

We all have expectations and dreams about everything we experience. To be honest, it is the driving force that helps us live. But how we expect is a matter we are all fancy about. Everything that we come across, we wanted them to happen in our life also. We may expect something small or big, either good or bad, satisfying or something unearthly. But still, we all expect.

However, as we delve deeper into the human experience, we're reminded of the cautionary tale of Pandora's Box. According to the myth, Pandora's curiosity and expectation of what might be inside the box eventually got the better of her, and she opened it, releasing a multitude of evils into the world. This myth warns us about the risks of uncontrolled expectation, where our desires and curiosity can lead us down a path of destruction and chaos.

As we explore the complexities of expectation, we begin to realize that it's a delicate balance between hope and despair, between the promise of fulfillment and the risk of disappointment.

Ancient Wisdom on Expectation

Quran

"Whoever puts their trust in something, they will be sufficed."

Bhagavad Gita

"You are what your deep, driving desire is."

Bible

"Delight yourself in the present moment, and you will receive the desires of your heart."

Join me on this journey as we unravel the enigma of expectation, and discover the intricate dance between hope, desire, and reality.

As we reflect on the power of expectation, let's remember that we've been evolving for millions of years, and it's our expectations that have propelled us forward. Today is better than yesterday, and tomorrow will be far better than today. With our actions and efforts, we can make our expectations a reality.

But as we stand at the threshold of this realization, we're faced with a profound question: what is it that we're striving for? What is the underlying drive that fuels our expectations and pushes us to pursue our dreams?

Is it the pursuit of happiness, the thrill of achievement, or something more fundamental? Perhaps it's the desire to leave a lasting impact, to make a difference in the world, or to find our place in the grand tapestry of human existence.

As we ponder these questions, we begin to uncover a deeper truth – one that speaks to the very essence of our being. We start to realize that our expectations are not just fleeting desires, but are, in fact, connected to something far more profound...

...a sense of purpose.

XIII

PURPOSE OF LIFE : PASSION FOR LIFE

What if the key to unlocking our true potential, to living a life that's authentic, fulfilling, and impactful, lies at the intersection of five profound elements: finding our flow, that state of complete absorption and engagement; pursuing our passions, those activities that set our souls on fire; self-actualizing our dreams, realizing our full potential and becoming the best version of ourselves; making meaning, creating a sense of purpose and significance in our lives; and discovering our ikigai, our reason for being, that unique convergence of what we're good at, what we love, and what the world needs?

Can Passion Change the World?

As you ponder this question, remember that the purpose of life is not just about personal fulfillment, but also about the positive impact you can have on the world. To you, the purpose of life is about reciprocating, being kind, and lovely. It's about being true to yourself, embracing your authenticity, and living with intention.

From Survival to Celebration

You often get caught up in the idea that life is just about survival, but what if you could transform your existence into a celebration of life? What if you could cherish every moment, savor every experience, and make the world a brighter, more compassionate place?

The Spark That Ignites

As Robert Frost so eloquently put it, "I have promises to keep, and miles to go before I sleep." These words resonate deeply within you, for you believe that your life is not just a series of mundane routines, but a tapestry of promises waiting to be fulfilled. Promises to yourself, to your loved ones, and to the world at large.

Tapping into the Qi of Interconnectedness

Life's passion is the driving force that transforms your existence from mere survival to a vibrant, thriving experience. It's the spark that ignites your creativity, fuels your imagination, and propels you toward your dreams. By embracing your passions, you tap into the Qi of Interconnectedness – the vital energy that flows through all living things, connecting you to the natural world, your communities, and yourself.

As you embark on this journey of self-discovery and growth, remember that:

- You are capable of unlocking your true potential.
- Your passions and purposes are worthy of pursuit.
- You trust yourself to make choices that align with your values and goals.
- You are connected to something greater than yourself.
- You choose to live a life driven by passion and purpose.

Embracing Your True Nature

As you continue on this journey, it's essential to take action and make intentional choices that align with your values and passions. You must challenge your own limitations and obstacles, and reframe your mindset to focus on progress, not perfection. You must prioritize your time and energy, and make space for activities that bring you joy and fulfillment.

Guiding Affirmations

- You trust yourself to make choices that align with your values and passions.
- You are capable of overcoming any obstacle that comes your way.
- You prioritize your time and energy, and make space for activities that bring you joy and fulfillment.
- You are worthy of pursuing your passions, and making a meaningful impact in the world.
- You are connected to something greater than yourself, and you trust in the universe's plan for your life.
- You choose to live a life driven by passion and purpose, and you are committed to making it a reality.

Is the purpose of life living and letting live, and the passion of life wanting to make a meaningful life? At any point, will it get compared, or will it offend our self-esteem? Let's voyage to find the island of wisdom that's hidden within us.

XIV
SELF-ESTEEM AND COMPARISON

The Journey of Self-Discovery: Navigating the Waters of Self-Esteem

As we embark on the winding river of life, our self-esteem flows like the gentle currents, shaping and reshaping itself with each twist and turn. Along the way, we encounter the turbulent waters of comparison, where the undertows of self-doubt and insecurity threaten to pull us under.

Yet, just as the river adapts to the landscape, carving out new paths and depths, we too can learn to navigate the complexities of life. We can cultivate the resilience of the Bamboo Tree, bending but never breaking in the face of adversity. This majestic tree, native to Asia, reminds us that flexibility and adaptability are essential for building dignity and preserving self-esteem.

As we navigate the complexities of life, we're confronted with the internal struggle between two wolves. This ancient Native American parable teaches us that one wolf represents our positive qualities – compassion, empathy, and kindness – while the other wolf embodies our negative traits – anger, jealousy, and resentment. The wolf that we feed will ultimately determine the trajectory of our life.

The Comparison Trap: Understanding the Impact on Self-Esteem

Comparison is a subtle yet insidious thief, stealing away our self-esteem and leaving us feeling inadequate and insecure. When we constantly measure ourselves against others, we create a false narrative that our worth is determined by external validation. But the truth is, comparison is a flawed metric for self-worth. This concept is echoed in the Buddhist teachings of mindfulness, which encourage us to focus on our own path rather than comparing ourselves to others.

Cultivating Self-Esteem: Building a Strong Foundation

Dignity is the foundation upon which self-esteem is built. When we prioritize our own dignity, we create a sense of self-worth that is unwavering and unshakeable. This concept of dignity is rooted in the ancient Greek philosophy of Stoicism, which emphasizes the importance of self-respect and inner strength. By building dignity, we create a protective barrier around our self-esteem, shielding it from the negative impacts of comparison and criticism.

To break free from the comparison trap and cultivate a stronger sense of self-esteem, we must focus on our own journey, celebrating our successes and learning from our setbacks. We must cultivate a sense of self-awareness, acknowledging our flaws and imperfections, but also recognizing our resilience and capacity for growth.

Just as the Lotus Flower blooms in the muddy waters, yet remains unsoiled, we too can emerge from life's challenges with our true beauty and worth intact. This ancient Egyptian symbol of rebirth and spiritual growth reminds us that our true strength lies within. The story of Emperor Ashoka, an Indian emperor who converted to Buddhism and promoted peace and tolerance, serves as a powerful reminder that it's never too late to change our path and cultivate a stronger sense of dignity and self-esteem.

As we continue on this journey, we'll encounter the transformational power of self-reflection and personal growth. We'll learn to prioritize our own dignity and self-worth, embracing the ever-changing landscape of life with courage, curiosity, and compassion. And when the storms of self-doubt and comparison rage on, we'll find shelter in the wisdom of the ages, reminding us that our true strength lies not in external validation, but in the depths of our own hearts and minds.

As we continue on this journey, we'll encounter the transformational power of self-reflection and personal growth. We'll learn to prioritize our own dignity and self-worth, embracing the ever-changing landscape of life with courage, curiosity, and compassion. And when the storms of self-doubt and comparison rage on, we'll find shelter in the wisdom of the ages, reminding us that our true strength lies not in external validation, but in the depths of our own hearts and minds.

In the stillness of the moment, we may catch a glimpse of our true selves – imperfect, yet perfectly whole. We may realize that the journey of self-discovery is not about arriving at a destination, but about embracing the beauty of the journey itself.

Reflections for the Journey Ahead

- What are the turbulent waters of comparison that you've encountered in your own life? How have they impacted your self-esteem?
- What are the qualities that make you unique and worthy of love and respect? How can you cultivate and celebrate these qualities?
- What is one step you can take today to prioritize your own dignity and self-worth?
- How can you practice self-compassion and kindness when faced with self-doubt and criticism?

These reflections are designed to be a starting point for your own journey of self-discovery. May they guide you as you navigate the waters of self-esteem and emerge stronger, wiser, and more compassionate.

XV
UNFILTERED &
UNAPOLOGETIC

Unleashing Your True Self: The Power of Being Unfiltered

Imagine living a life where you can be radically honest with yourself and others, without fear of judgment or rejection. A life where you can shed the masks and pretenses, and simply be yourself.

This is the life of the unfiltered, where vulnerability is not a weakness, but a strength. When we dare to be ourselves, we open ourselves up to a world of possibilities.

Embracing the Beauty of Imperfection

We no longer have to conform to societal standards of perfection, and instead, can celebrate our unique quirks and flaws. This is the beauty of imperfection, where our rough edges and scars become the very things that make us beautiful.

But what does it take to live this kind of life? It takes courage, resilience, and a willingness to be vulnerable. It takes a commitment to radical honesty, even when it's hard or uncomfortable.

And Now, It's Time to Take It to the Next Level...

Being unapologetic is not just about being true to yourself, but also about embracing your worth and value without apology or justification.

The Unapologetic Revolution

Imagine living a life where you can express yourself authentically, without fear of judgment or rejection. A life where you can stand confidently in your truth, without seeking external validation or approval.

This is the life of the unapologetic, where your existence, opinions, and experiences are valid and deserving of respect. Your existence is not a mistake. You have the right to take up space, express yourself, and live your life without apology.

Owning Your Worth

To embody this unapologetic mindset, it's crucial to recognize and honor your self-worth. This means acknowledging your strengths, weaknesses, and quirks, and accepting yourself exactly as you are.

It's about standing in your worth, confidently asserting your value and worth without seeking external validation or approval. Setting boundaries is also essential to being unapologetic.

Speaking Your Truth

This means establishing and maintaining healthy limits with others to protect your time, energy, and emotional well-being. It's about communicating your needs, wants, and opinions clearly and respectfully, without aggression or passivity.

For instance, imagine being in a situation where someone asks for your opinion, and you feel hesitant to share it. Instead of apologizing or downplaying your thoughts, you confidently express yourself, saying, "I appreciate your question, and here's my honest opinion...."

Unapologetic and Unstoppable

By embracing these universal truths and principles, you can cultivate an unapologetic mindset and live a life that is authentic, empowered, and fulfilling.

You'll be able to:

- Recognize and honor your inherent worth and value
- Express yourself authentically, without apology or justification
- Set healthy boundaries to protect your time, energy, and emotional well-being
- Communicate your needs, wants, and opinions clearly and respectfully
- Stand confidently in your truth, without seeking external validation or approval

As you embark on this journey, remember that embracing your authentic self is a powerful act of self-love, self-acceptance, and self-empowerment.

The Unapologetic Challenge

Are you ready to unleash your unfiltered and unapologetic self? Are you ready to live a life that is authentic, empowered, and fulfilling?

Then join the unapologetic revolution, and discover the power of being true to yourself, without apology or justification.

XVI
EMBRACING YOUR AUTHETIC SELF

As we journey through life, we wear many hats. We're a child, full of wonder and curiosity. We're a student, striving to learn and grow. We're a sibling, navigating the complexities of family dynamics. We're a parent, guiding and nurturing the next generation. We're a professional, pursuing our passions and building our careers.

But in the midst of these various roles, we often forget to be ourselves. We conform to societal expectations, hiding our true nature behind masks of pretension. Yet, as the ancient Greeks inscribed on the Temple of Apollo at Delphi, "Know Thyself". This phrase emphasizes the importance of self-awareness and understanding one's own nature.

In Buddhist philosophy, the concept of "The Unconditioned Self" refers to the true, authentic self that exists beyond conditioning and societal expectations. As the Buddha taught, "The mind is everything; what you think, you become." By letting go of external expectations and focusing on our inner selves, we can uncover our authentic nature. This process of self-discovery requires patience, mindfulness, and a willingness to confront our deepest fears and insecurities. As the Buddha said, "You yourself, as much as anybody in the entire universe, deserve your love and affection."

Taoist philosophy also emphasizes the importance of embracing one's true self. The concept of "Wu Wei" encourages us to take action without forcing or pretending. As Lao Tzu wrote, "Nature does not hurry, yet everything is accomplished." By aligning ourselves with our natural flow, we can live more authentically. This means embracing our imperfections, quirks, and flaws, and recognizing that they are an integral part of our unique identity. As Lao Tzu said, "The Tao does nothing, and yet nothing is left undone."

In African culture, the proverb "When you pray, move your feet" emphasizes taking action towards being true to oneself and living authentically. This means being proactive in pursuing our passions and values, rather than waiting for external validation or approval. Another proverb, "The world is a looking glass, and gives back to every man the reflection of his own face," highlights the importance of self-awareness and being true to oneself. This means recognizing that our external circumstances are often a reflection of our internal state, and taking responsibility for creating the life we desire.

Native American wisdom also offers valuable insights on embracing one's authentic self. The saying "Be as a tree, and let the dead leaves drop" encourages letting go of what's no longer needed and embracing one's true nature. This means releasing attachment to external expectations, and instead, focusing on our inner wisdom and intuition. Another saying, "Listen to the whispers of your heart," emphasizes the importance of listening to one's intuition and being true to oneself. This means trusting our inner guidance, and having the courage to follow our hearts, even when it means going against the status quo.

As we embark on this journey of self-discovery, remember that embracing your authentic self requires courage, vulnerability, and a willingness to take risks. It means:- Letting go of the need for external validation and approval
- Embracing your imperfections, quirks, and flaws.

-Standing up for yourself, your values, and your boundariesAs the ancient wisdom of the ages converges with the beating of your heart, remember that embracing your authentic self is an act of sacred rebellion. It's a declaration of independence from the expectations of others, and a celebration of the freedom to be yourself. In the stillness of the moment, listen to the whispers of your soul. It's the voice of your authentic self, guiding you home to the truth of who you are. By embracing this truth, you'll unlock the gates of your potential, and the world will be transformed by the radiance of your authenticity.

So, rise up, dear one, and let the majesty of your authentic self illuminate the world. Take the first step, and watch as the universe conspires to support the magnificent unfolding of your true self.

As you embark on this journey of self-discovery, remember to be gentle with yourself, to trust your intuition, and to celebrate your uniqueness. Embracing your authentic self is a courageous act of self-love, and it's the key to unlocking your full potential.

By embracing your true self, you'll break free from the shackles of societal expectations, and you'll discover a sense of purpose, belonging, and fulfillment that's been waiting to be unleashed. So, take a deep breath, be brave, and let your authenticity shine!

XVII
BEYOND ENVY

Envy is a universal human emotion, but it can also be a destructive force in our lives and relationships. In this chapter, we'll explore the root causes of envy, its consequences, and most importantly, how to overcome it.

The Root of Envy

Envy is often confused with jealousy, but they are distinct emotions. Jealousy is the fear of losing something we already possess, whereas envy is the desire for something someone else possesses. Envy can stem from insecurity, low self-esteem, or feelings of inadequacy.

Societal pressures and social media can fuel envy. We're constantly bombarded with curated images and success stories, making it easy to compare and feel inferior. However, it's essential to remember that everyone's journey is unique, and comparisons are unfair to ourselves and others.

The Impact of Envy on Our Lives

Envy can have far-reaching consequences, affecting various aspects of our lives:

- Career: Envy can lead to unhealthy competition, sabotage, and burnout. It can also prevent us from forming meaningful connections with colleagues and mentors.
- Education: Envy can create a toxic learning environment, where students feel pressured to compete rather than collaborate. It can also lead to academic dishonesty and a lack of personal growth.
- Peaceful Living: Envy can rob us of our peace and happiness. When we're constantly comparing ourselves to others, we can never truly be content with our own lives.

- Healthy Relationships: Envy can damage our relationships with others. When we envy someone, we often focus on their strengths and our weaknesses, creating a distorted view of reality.

Overcoming Envy

Recognizing envy is the first step to overcoming it. Take time to reflect on your feelings and identify the root causes of your envy. Ask yourself:

- What triggers my envy?
- What am I afraid of losing or not having?
- What are my strengths and weaknesses?

Practicing gratitude and empathy can also help overcome envy. Focus on the things you're thankful for, and try to understand others' perspectives and struggles.

Cultivating a Culture of Support

Creating a supportive environment where people feel encouraged, not envied, is crucial. Here are some actionable tips:

- Celebrate others' successes and acknowledge their hard work.
- Offer constructive feedback and support.
- Focus on your own journey and progress.
- Practice empathy and understanding.

By moving beyond envy, we can build stronger, more meaningful relationships, achieve our goals, and cultivate a positive, supportive community.

Rising Above Envy

Remember that envy is a natural human emotion, but it's also a choice. We can choose to let envy consume us, or we can rise above it.

Envy may seem like a harmless emotion, but it can have far-reaching consequences, affecting our relationships, career, education, and overall well-being. It can prevent us from forming genuine connections with others, achieving our goals, and living a peaceful, fulfilling life.

However, by recognizing the root causes of envy, practicing gratitude and empathy, and cultivating a culture of support, we can overcome envy and unlock our full potential.

Rising above envy requires self-awareness, self-reflection, and a willingness to change. It requires us to focus on our own journey, celebrate others' successes, and cultivate meaningful relationships.

As you move forward, remember that you are not alone in this journey. Everyone struggles with envy at some point in their lives. But it's how we respond to envy that matters.

So, choose to rise above envy. Choose to focus on your strengths, celebrate others' successes, and cultivate a culture of support. Choose to live a life that's authentic, empowering, and transformative.

By doing so, you'll not only overcome envy but also unlock a more fulfilling, purpose-driven life. A life where you can build stronger, more meaningful relationships, achieve your goals, and live with peace, happiness, and contentment.

XVIII
GRATITUDE UNLOCKS

GRATITUDE UNLOCKS

Gratitude is a powerful emotion that can transform our lives and relationships. It's a feeling that can bring us joy, comfort, and a sense of connection to others. In this chapter, we'll explore the benefits of gratitude, its universal significance, and practical ways to cultivate it.

The Power of Gratitude

Gratitude is more than just a feeling; it's a practice that can have a profound impact on our well-being. Research has shown that gratitude can:

- Improve mental health and resilience: Gratitude has been linked to lower levels of stress, anxiety, and depression. It can also help us develop a more optimistic outlook and improve our overall mental health.
- Strengthen relationships and build stronger bonds: When we express gratitude towards others, it can strengthen our relationships and build trust. It can also help us communicate more effectively and resolve conflicts in a more positive way.
- Increase empathy and compassion: Gratitude can help us develop a more empathetic and compassionate attitude towards others. When we focus on the good things in our lives, we're more likely to be kind and understanding towards others.
- Enhance physical health and well-being: Gratitude has been linked to better physical health, including lower blood pressure, stronger immune systems, and fewer chronic illnesses.
- Foster a sense of purpose and meaning: Gratitude can help us develop a sense of purpose and meaning in our lives. When we focus on the things we're thankful for, we're more likely to feel connected to something larger

than ourselves.

Universal Significance of Gratitude

Gratitude is a universal value that transcends cultures and traditions. Here are some examples:

India: Hinduism and Gratitude

In Hinduism, gratitude is considered a sacred duty . This concept emphasizes the importance of acknowledging and expressing gratitude towards others, especially towards those who have helped us or provided for us.

The festival of Makar Sankranti, celebrated in January, is a prime example of gratitude in Hinduism. The festival marks the beginning of the sun's journey towards the northern hemisphere and is a celebration of the harvest season. During this festival, people express gratitude for the sun's warmth and light, which is essential for the growth and prosperity of crops.

Islam and Gratitude

In Islam, gratitude is considered a fundamental virtue and is expressed through the concept of "shukr" (gratitude). Muslims are encouraged to express gratitude towards Allah for the blessings and favors they have received.

The Quran emphasizes the importance of gratitude, stating, "And remember when your Lord proclaimed, 'If you are grateful, I will surely increase you [in favor]'" (Quran 14:7). Muslims are encouraged to express gratitude through prayer, charity, and good deeds.

Christianity and Gratitude

In Christianity, gratitude is considered a fundamental virtue and is expressed through the concept of "thanksgiving." Christians are encouraged to express gratitude towards God for the blessings and favors they have received.

The Bible emphasizes the importance of gratitude, stating, "Give thanks to the Lord, for he is good; his love endures forever!" (Psalm 107:1). Christians are encouraged to express gratitude through prayer, worship, and good deeds.

Greece: Aristotle and Gratitude

Greek philosophy emphasizes the importance of gratitude. The Greek philosopher Aristotle considered gratitude a virtue, essential for building strong relationships and a healthy society. In his work "Nicomachean Ethics," Aristotle emphasized the importance of gratitude as a means of cultivating friendships and social bonds.

China: Confucianism and Gratitude

In Confucianism, gratitude is seen as a key aspect of ren (benevolence) and is considered essential for maintaining social harmony. Confucius emphasized the importance of gratitude as a means of cultivating virtues and promoting social relationships.

Korea: Jeong and Gratitude

In Korean culture, gratitude is expressed through the concept of "jeong" (deep emotional connection and gratitude). Jeong refers to the deep emotional bonds that exist between individuals, often characterized by feelings of gratitude, loyalty, and affection.

America: Thanksgiving and Gratitude

The tradition of Thanksgiving in the United States is a celebration of gratitude for the harvest season and the blessings of life. The holiday, celebrated on the fourth Thursday of November, originated in 1621 when the Pilgrims held a harvest feast to express gratitude for their first successful crop.

Cultivating Gratitude

So, how can we cultivate gratitude in our daily lives? Here are some practical tips:

- Keep a gratitude journal: Writing down the things we're thankful for can help us focus on the positive aspects of our lives. Try to write in your journal every day, no matter how small the things you're grateful for may seem.
- Share gratitude with others: Expressing gratitude towards others can strengthen our relationships and build trust. Try to thank someone every day, whether it's a kind word, a text message, or a small gift.
- Practice mindfulness and presence: Mindfulness and presence can help us appreciate the beauty around us. Try to focus on the present moment, without judgment or distraction.
- Celebrate the small wins and joys in life: Celebrating the small things in life can help us cultivate a sense of gratitude and appreciation. Try to celebrate something every day, no matter how small it may seem.
- Show appreciation for the people and relationships in your life: The people and relationships in our lives are often the things we're most grateful for. Try to show appreciation for them every day, whether it's a kind word, a hug, or a small gift.

Gratitude is a powerful force that can unlock happiness, resilience, and stronger relationships. By cultivating gratitude, we can create a more positive, compassionate, and harmonious world. Remember, gratitude is a practice that takes time and effort to develop. Start small, be consistent, and watch how gratitude can transform your life.

Gratitude is a powerful force that can transform our lives, relationships, and communities. By cultivating gratitude, we can unlock happiness, resilience, and stronger relationships.

Gratitude becomes a powerful catalyst for transformation when we embody it as a way of life. As we weave gratitude into the fabric of our daily experiences, we begin to notice a profound shift in our perspective, relationships, and overall well-being. With each passing day, we become more resilient, compassionate, and connected to the world around us.

What are you grateful for today?

XIX
FORGIVENESS FOUND

Forgiveness Found

As we navigate through life's pages, we're reminded that we're perfectly imperfect. We've made mistakes, stumbled, and fallen. But where can we seek forgiveness? How can we release the weight of our past errors and move forward with hope and renewal?

The Weight of Unforgiveness

Unforgiveness can be a heavy burden, pulling us down and preventing us from reaching our full potential. It's a weight that can suffocate us, making it difficult to breathe, to live, and to love. But we don't have to carry this burden alone.

Seeking Forgiveness

So, where can we seek forgiveness? The answer lies within ourselves and in the relationships we build with others.

Forgiving Ourselves

The first step towards forgiveness is to forgive ourselves. We must acknowledge our mistakes, take responsibility for our actions, and release the guilt and shame that often accompany our errors. Forgiving ourselves is not easy, but it's essential for healing and moving forward.

Forgiving Others

The next step is to forgive others. This can be even more challenging, especially when we feel hurt, betrayed, or wronged. But forgiveness is not about the other person; it's about us. When we forgive others, we release the negative emotions associated with the hurt, and we create space for healing and growth.

The Power of Forgiveness

Forgiveness is a powerful tool that can transform our lives and relationships. When we forgive, we:

- Release the weight of unforgiveness
- Create space for healing and growth
- Improve our mental and emotional well-being
- Strengthen our relationships with others
- Increase our sense of empathy and compassion

Letting Go of the Past

As we forgive ourselves and others, we must also let go of the past. We can't change what's happened, but we can change how we respond to it. We can choose to hold onto the past, or we can release it and move forward.

Living in the Present

Forgiveness allows us to live in the present moment, free from the burdens of the past. When we forgive, we create space for new experiences, new relationships, and new opportunities.

The Complexity of Forgiveness

Forgiveness is a complex and multifaceted concept that has been debated by philosophers, theologians, and scholars across various disciplines. Some argue that forgiveness is a moral obligation, while others contend that it's a personal choice. This debate raises important questions about the nature of forgiveness and its relationship to morality, justice, and personal freedom.

Forgiving the Unforgivable

Another philosophical debate surrounding forgiveness centers on whether it's possible to forgive extreme wrongdoing, such as genocide or torture. Can we forgive those who have caused irreparable harm and suffering? Or are some actions so heinous that they're unforgivable? This debate challenges us to confront the limits of forgiveness and the nature of evil.

Forgiveness and Justice

Some philosophers argue that forgiveness can be incompatible with justice, as it may involve letting wrongdoers off the hook. However, others contend that forgiveness can be a powerful tool for restorative justice, allowing individuals and communities to heal and rebuild. This debate highlights the complex relationship between forgiveness, justice, and morality.

The Role of Mercy and Compassion

Mercy and compassion are essential components of forgiveness. Mercy involves showing compassion and forgiveness towards others, often in situations where they're deserving of punishment. Compassion involves feeling empathy and concern for others, which can be a key component of forgiveness. By cultivating mercy and compassion, we can create a more forgiving and compassionate world.

Restorative Justice and Forgiveness

Restorative justice involves repairing harm caused by wrongdoing, which can involve forgiveness and reconciliation. This approach prioritizes healing and reparation over punishment and retribution. By embracing restorative justice, we can create a more just and forgiving society.

A Message to You

As you step out of my book and into your life as an adult, remember that forgiveness is a journey. It's not always easy, but it's essential for growth, healing, and transformation. Don't hold onto grudges or past hurts. Instead, choose to forgive yourself and others. Let your actions speak to who you are, and always remember that you are capable of growth, change, and transformation.

From Darkness to Light

Forgiveness is the bridge that spans the chasm between darkness and light. As we forgive, we cross over from the shadows of our past into the radiant light of our future. This journey of forgiveness leaves a legacy of love, a testament to the human spirit's capacity for compassion and kindness.

The Gift of Forgiveness

Forgiveness is a gift, a precious treasure that we can give to ourselves and others. As we forgive, we receive the gift of peace, joy, and liberation. This gift has the power to revolutionize our lives, our relationships, and our world.

The Freedom to Forgive

Forgiveness is a choice, a decision to break free from the chains of resentment and anger. As we forgive, we claim our freedom, our power to choose love over hate. This freedom creates a ripple effect, touching hearts and lives far beyond our own.

A New Dawn

Forgiveness brings a new dawn, a chance to start anew. As we forgive, we rise above the ashes of our past, reborn and renewed. With every step towards forgiveness, we move closer to a brighter future, one filled with hope, love, and compassion.

Let's forgive and move forward, but not necessarily forget. Remembering our experiences, both good and bad, helps us learn and grow.

Forgiveness is about releasing the negative emotions associated with a past hurt or wrongdoing. It's about letting go of resentment, anger, and bitterness.

Forgetting, on the other hand, can be problematic. Forgetting can lead to repeating the same mistakes or patterns that led to hurt or harm in the first place.

Instead, let's strive for forgiveness and understanding. Let's learn from our experiences and use them to become wiser, more compassionate, and more empathetic individuals.

So, let's forgive, learn, and move forward with love, kindness, and wisdom!

XX

LEAVING A LASTING LEGACY: MAKING A MEANINGFUL IMPACT

As you close this book, remember that your journey is a rich and complex one, shaped by every experience, every lesson, and every relationship. Each moment, each decision, and each encounter has contributed to the person you are today.

You've discovered the spark of life that ignites your passions and purpose. This spark has guided you through the ups and downs of life, reminding you of your inner strength and resilience. You've learned valuable early lessons that shaped your perspective and approach to life, teaching you to adapt, to persevere, and to grow.

Education has played a vital role in your journey, empowering you with knowledge, skills, and critical thinking. You've come to realize that education is not just a fundamental right, but also a powerful tool for growth, transformation, and social change.

Through your journey, you've encountered mistakes and setbacks, but you've also learned to transform them into opportunities for growth and self-improvement. You've discovered the hope that lies within you, a hope that guides and motivates you to pursue your dreams, even in the face of adversity.

You've built meaningful relationships with friends and family, and you've learned to nurture and cherish them. You've understood the importance of embracing imperfections, both in yourself and in others, and of practicing self-compassion and self-forgiveness. You've learned to communicate effectively, to listen actively, and to resolve conflicts in a constructive and respectful manner.

You've mastered the art of saying no, setting healthy boundaries, and prioritizing your own needs and desires. You've learned to navigate the fragility of human connections and to cultivate resilience and adaptability in the face of change and uncertainty.

In a world dominated by social media, you've learned to critically evaluate the impact of technology on your life and relationships. You've come to understand the beauty and complexity of expectations, and you've discovered your purpose and passion in life. You've learned to balance your online and offline lives, to cultivate meaningful connections, and to prioritize your mental and emotional well-being.

Through your journey, you've developed a strong sense of self-esteem, unshaken by comparisons or external validation. You've learned to embrace your authentic self, unapologetically and unfiltered. You've risen beyond envy and negativity, and you've unlocked the transformative power of gratitude. You've discovered that true happiness and fulfillment come from within, and that you have the power to create the life you desire.

Finally, you've discovered the liberating power of forgiveness, freeing yourself from the burdens of the past and embracing a brighter, more hopeful future. You've learned to let go of grudges, to release negative emotions, and to cultivate compassion and empathy for yourself and others.

As you step out into the world, remember that you are a unique, talented, and resilient individual, capable of making a meaningful impact. Carry the lessons and insights from this journey with you, and share them with others. Leave a lasting legacy that inspires and uplifts those around you.

Remember to be kind, compassionate, and gentle with yourself and others. Remember to take risks, to challenge yourself, and to pursue your dreams with courage and determination.

You got this!

Voice Of the Journey

The journey of two decades has yielded valuable lessons. Resilience is key, and perseverance in the face of trauma and adversity is crucial. Self-awareness and authenticity are essential, as staying true to oneself is vital, even in challenging situations.

Setting boundaries is also crucial, as prioritizing self-care and protecting oneself from harm or exploitation is necessary. Moreover, navigating pain and hurt can foster compassion, empathy, and kindness towards others.

Life's unpredictability can be challenging, and expectations can be harmful. Accepting that life doesn't always go as planned and letting go of unrealistic expectations is essential. Focusing on what can be controlled and taking things one step at a time is a valuable approach.

Finally, understanding that replacement is a principle, not an emotion, can help navigate loss and heartache. People and relationships can be replaced, and this principle can facilitate moving forward.

These hard-won lessons offer valuable insights into life, resilience, and the importance of staying true to oneself.

I've shared my insights of journey, now it's time for me to step aside and let you navigate on your own path. Enjoiment is all yours!

Just a happy beginning

With all love...

RIZALY SIDDIQ